Field Trip

A Story About Sharing

Written by
Cindy Leaney

Illustrated by
Peter Wilks

Rourke
Publishing LLC
Vero Beach, Florida 32964

Before you read this story, take a look at the front cover of the book. The kids are visiting a zoo, and they are about to eat lunch.

1. Why is the girl in the background looking so unhappy?

2. How do you think sharing might be a part of the story?

Produced by SGA Illustration and Design
Designed by Phil Kay
Series Editor: Frank Sloan

www.rourkepublishing.com

Library of Congress Cataloging-in-Publication Data

Leaney, Cindy.
  Field trip : sharing / by Cindy Leaney ; illustrated by Peter Wilks.
     p. cm. -- (Hero club character)
  Summary: Matt and his classmates share their lunches with the new student, Ashley, because she has forgotten hers.
  ISBN 1-58952-734-8 (hardcover)
  1. Sharing. [1. Sharing. 2. Character.] I. Wilks, Peter, ill. II.
Title. III. Series: Leaney, Cindy. Hero club character.

LB1047.L39 2003
370.11'4--dc21

                              2003003590

Printed in the USA
MP/W

Welcome to The Hero Club!

Read about all the things that happen to them.

Try and guess what they'll do next.

www.theheroclub.com

"Where are you going on the field trip, Matt?"

"The Zoo and the Natural History Museum."

"Cool."

"Let's make sure you've got everything in your pack. Snack, lunch, jacket, notebook. Oh, and money for juice. Okay?"

"Okay!"

"Hi, José."

"Hi, Matt. There are Makayla and Emily."

8

"Let's sit together on the bus."

"Okay."

"Look at that! T Rex!"

"Look at that! A brontosaurus. Wow!"

"Come here a minute, you guys."

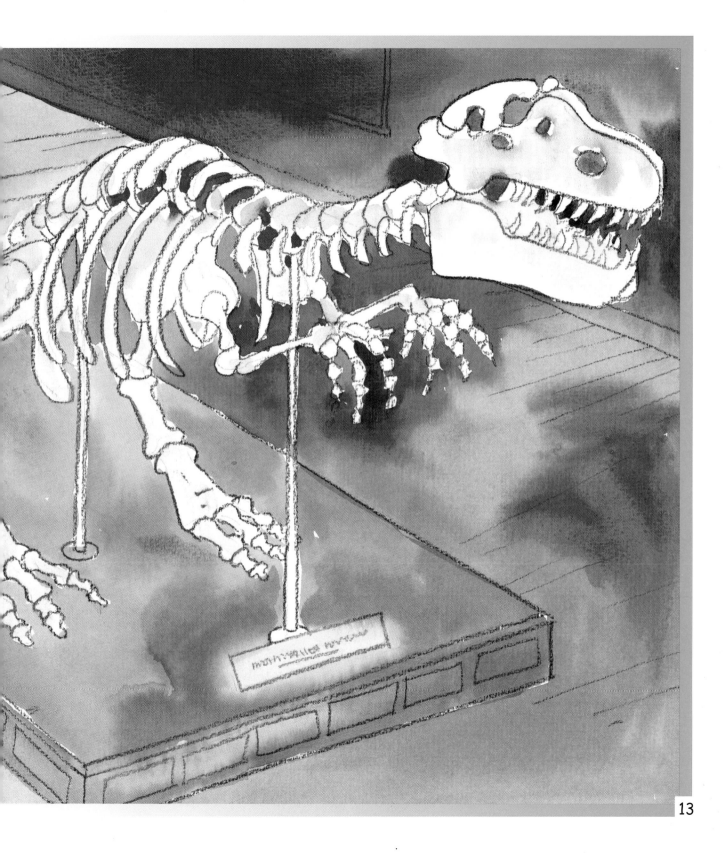

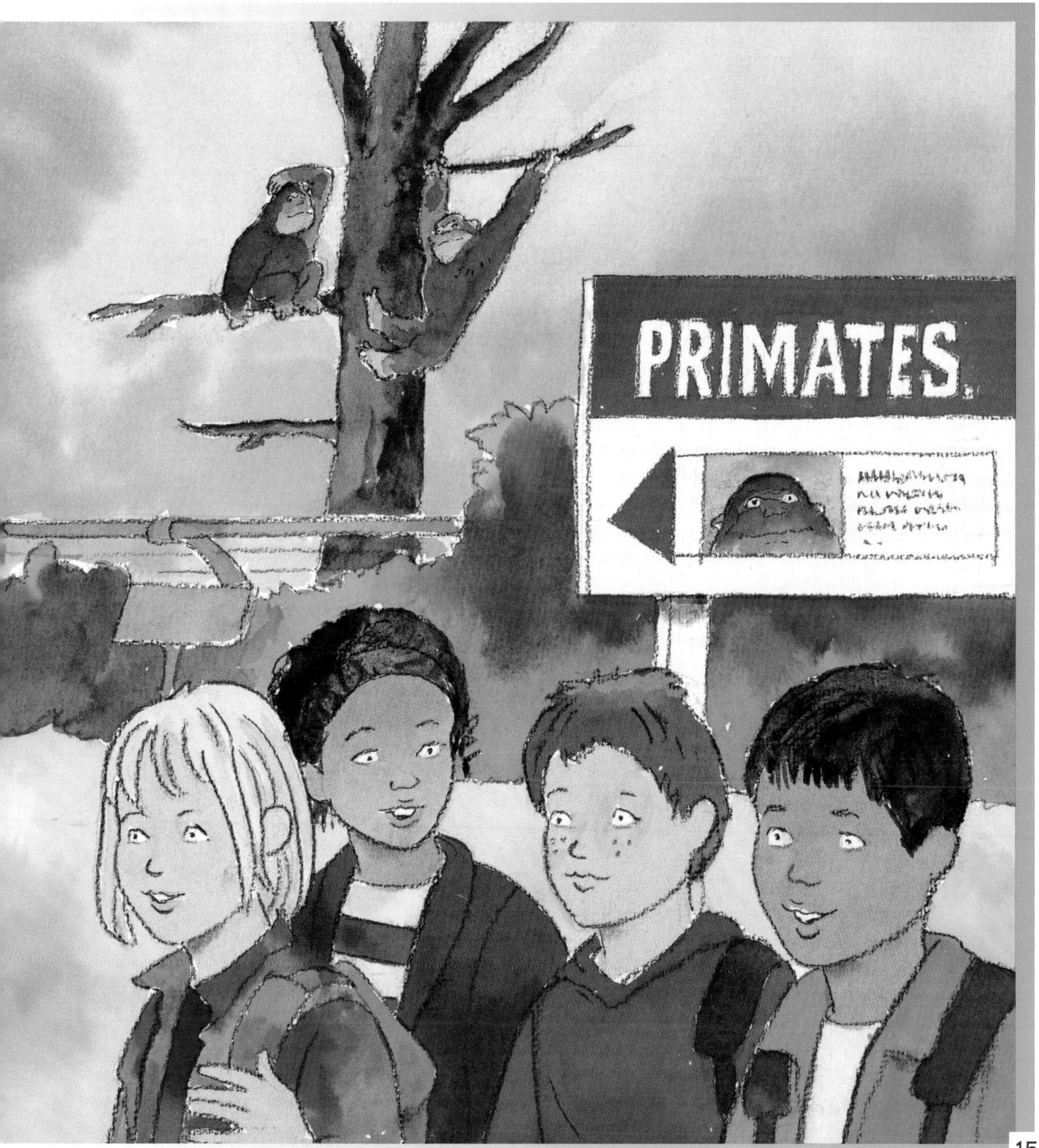
PRIMATES.

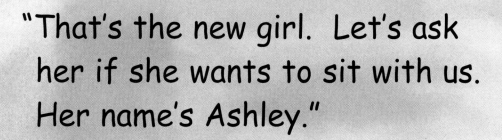

"That's the new girl. Let's ask her if she wants to sit with us. Her name's Ashley."

"Ashley, come and eat lunch with us."

"That's okay.
We've got lots.
You can have some
of ours."

"Do you like peanut butter, Ashley?"

"Here, let's put stuff in the middle.
Then we can all help ourselves."

"I've got celery and carrots."

"I've got some grapes."

24

"Ashley forgot her lunch so
we're all sharing."

"Way to go, kids."

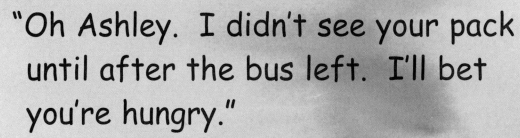

"Oh Ashley. I didn't see your pack until after the bus left. I'll bet you're hungry."

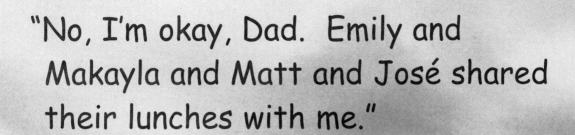

"No, I'm okay, Dad. Emily and Makayla and Matt and José shared their lunches with me."

"Thanks, kids. How about an ice cream cone for dessert? My treat!"

WHAT DO YOU THINK?

How were the Hero Kids generous on the field trip?

IMPORTANT IDEAS

Generous – A generous person is kind and gives time and things freely. The opposite of generous is selfish. Selfish people only care about themselves, not other people.

Share – To let someone use or have something of yours. On page 27 Ashley says,

"Emily and Makayla and Matt and José shared their lunches with me."

Is sharing easy or hard to do? Why?

Now that you have read this book, see if you can answer these questions:

1. What does Matt have in his pack when he sets off on the field trip?

2. What kinds of food do the Hero Club kids share with Ashley?

3. How does the teacher react when she finds that the Hero Club kids have shared their lunches with Ashley?

4. What does Ashley's father want to give the Hero Club kids because they shared their lunch with Ashley?

About the author

Cindy Leaney teaches English and writes books for both young readers and adults. She has lived and worked in England, Kenya, Mexico, Saudi Arabia, and the United States.

About the illustrator

Peter Wilks began work in advertising, where he developed a love for illustration. He has drawn pictures for many children's books in Great Britain and in the United States.

HERO CLUB CHARACTER VALUE SERIES

Everyone Makes a Difference (A Book About Community)

Field Trip (A Book About Sharing)

It's Your Turn Now (A Book About Politeness)

Lost and Found (A Book About Honesty)

Summer Vacation (A Book About Patience)

Taking Care of Mango (A Book About Responsibility)